beanz books

Alice's Wonderful Hospital Adventure

By Tony Densley and Niki Palmer

This book belongs to

....

First Edition 2019
ISBN: 978-1-925422-20-7
Author Tony Densley and Niki Palmer
Illustrated by Daniel Aires

With thanks to Dr Andrew Davies who reviewed this book, and Emma Davies who provided valuable insights from a child's perspective.

Alice's adventure to the hospital is about to begin.

Alice has not been feeling well for a couple of days. Her tummy has become sore, and the Doctor tells her Mummy that Alice will need to go to the hospital so that the doctors and nurses can help her to feel better.

Alice has not been to a hospital before, and this is a big adventure for her. Mummy tells her she will have an operation to remove her appendix.

Alice doesn't know what that is, but she knows that it hurts her tummy a lot. She is glad to be having it taken out.

Alice is not sure what to take with her to the hospital. She knows that Teddy will need to come with her, as she sleeps with Teddy in her bed every night.

What special things do you think Alice should take to the hospital?

Her pyjamas?

A special blanket?

Perhaps her favourite storybook!

When Alice arrives at the hospital, a lovely nurse meets her and Mummy and takes them into a little room.

The nurse gives her a special gown to wear and a white plastic bracelet.

The bracelet has Alice's name on it, so everyone knows who she is.

Alice sees many sick children while she is in hospital. Some of them walk on crutches, some are in wheelchairs, and some of them don't have any hair.

Why do you think the other children are there?

Perhaps they have broken their leg or arm.

Maybe they are having an operation, just like Alice!

The hospital may smell funny too, that is because there can't be any yucky germs in the hospital, so everything must be very, very clean.

People need to clean their hands with a special gel when they come to the hospital, so they keep the germs away.

This yucky germ doesn't like the idea of being clean.

Alice also sees a lot of funny machines, both big and small. Some machines make strange sounds like 'Beep beep' and 'Boop boop'.

Some even make funny sucking noises, just like when you suck through a straw.

Some of the machines have long wires and tubes that are attached to the children in bed.

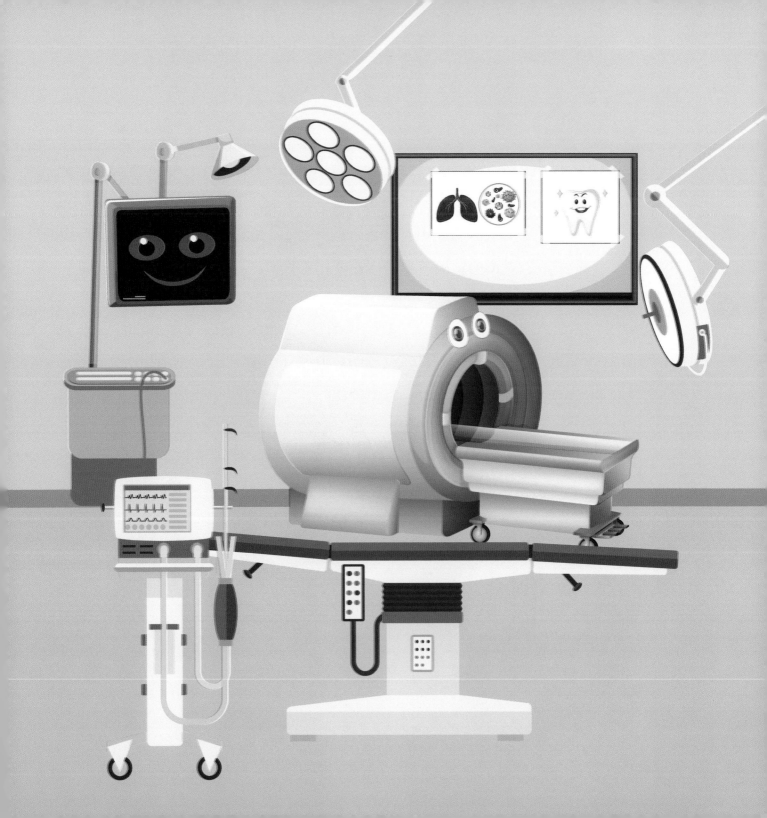

Alice waits until the doctor is ready to do her operation. While Alice waits, she is taken to a room to have an x-ray or ultrasound on her tummy. Alice lays very still while a special camera, which can see through people's bodies, has a look at her tummy.

The nurses may also put an IV drip into Alice's hand or arm. The IV drip looks like a thin little straw, and this gives Alice some medicine before, during and after the operation.

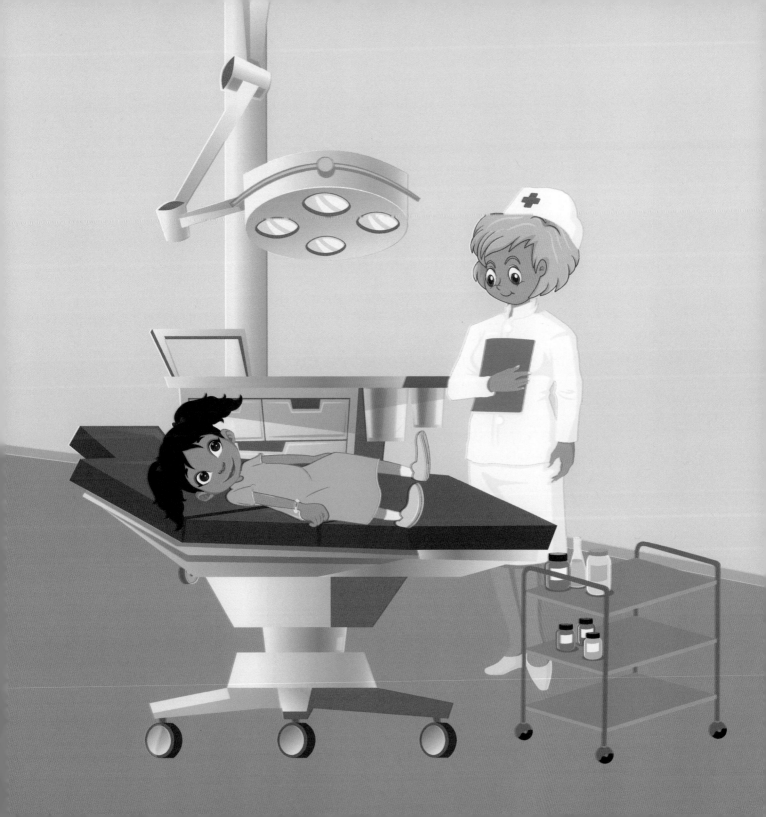

The nurses show Alice and Mummy to the big room Alice will sleep in, it is called a ward.

Other children are in bed there too. Some have already had their operation, and some are waiting just like Alice.

Can you count the number of children in Alice's room?

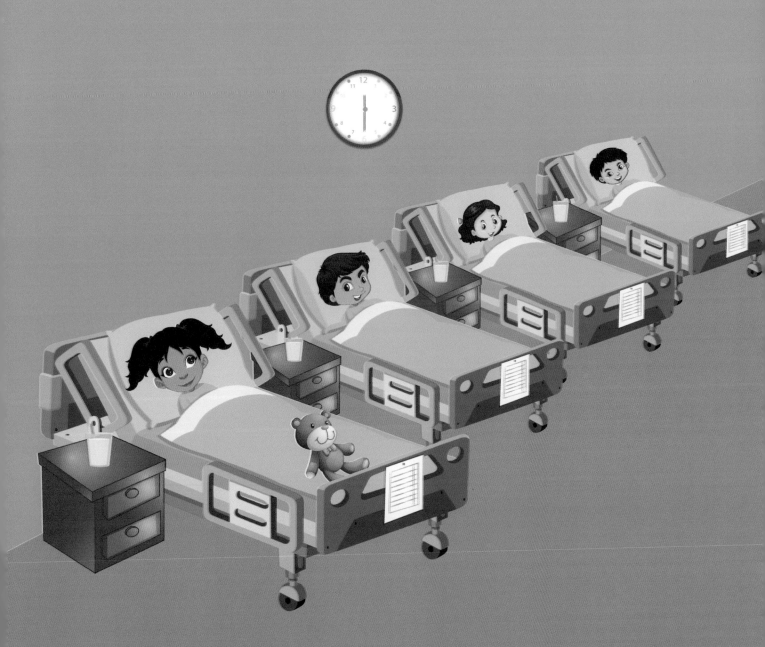

There is a big bed for Alice to lie in. It is a special bed on wheels. Alice presses a switch to move the bed up and down. This helps Alice to feel comfortable.

Alice shows her mummy how it works, and they laugh when she has her legs up and her head down.

Mummy stays with Alice, right up until she goes to sleep for the operation.

Many different doctors work in a hospital. The doctor who performs Alice's operation is called a surgeon. Her name is Doctor Jessica.

Doctor Jessica listens to Alice's heart with a special gadget called a stethoscope (steth-o-scope). The long tubes fit into the doctor's ears, and the metal piece is placed on her Alice's chest.

The doctor lets Alice listen as well!

What do you think Alice's heart sounds like?

Thump, thump… thump, thump… thump thump!

Who else do you think will come to see Alice?

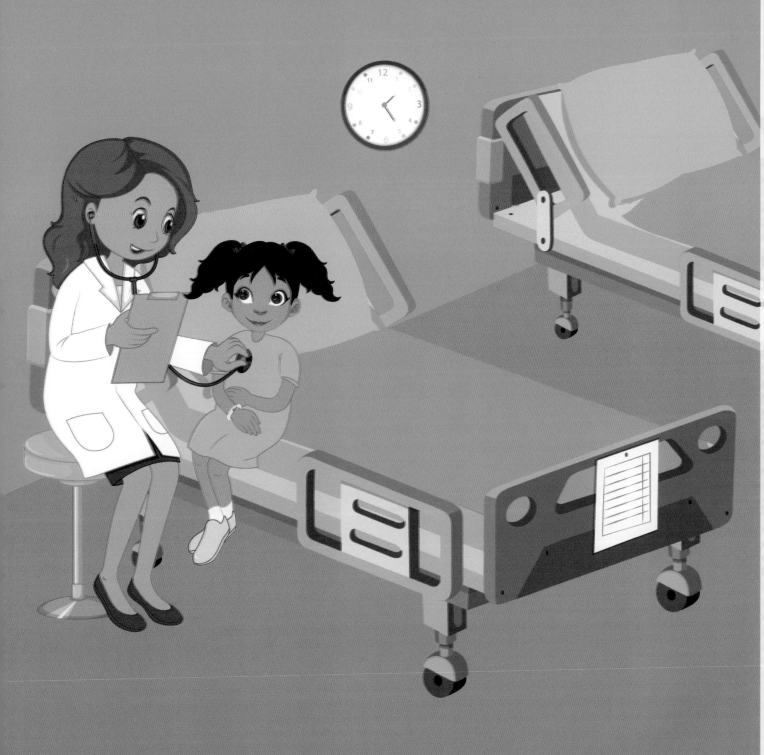

The friendly nurses often visit to make sure Alice is all right, as she must wait a long time before her operation.

While they take her temperature and blood pressure with special gadgets, she has to sit very still.

What could Alice do while she waits for her operation?

Play with mummy? Read a story? Play eye-spy? Sing a song?

Talk to the other children?

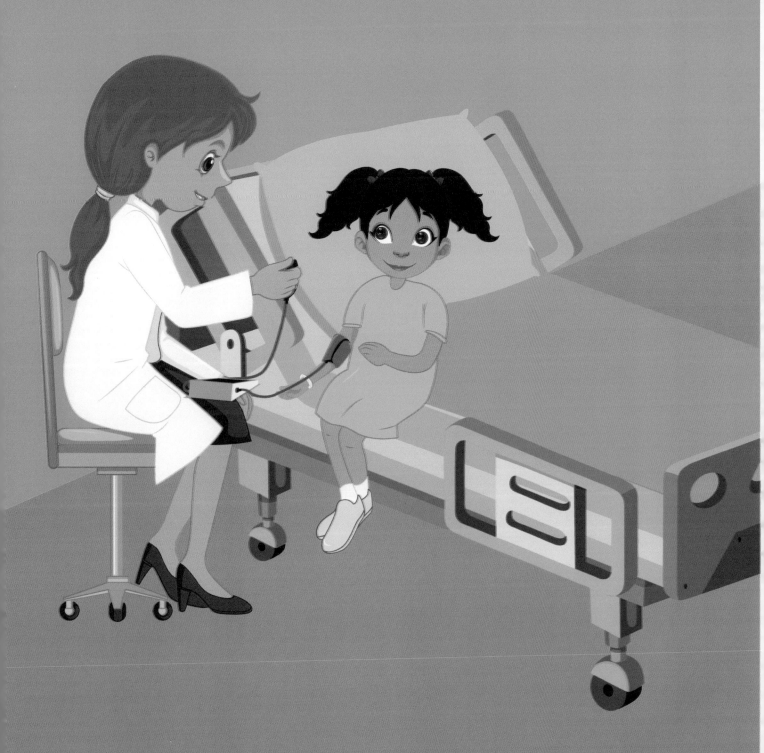

Now the time has come for Alice's operation. She lies in her bed with wheels, while a friendly porter takes her to a room next to the operating theatre. Mummy goes with her too and will stay with her until the operation.

Alice is lying down as she goes into the lift… it feels like she is on a roller coaster right there in the hospital!

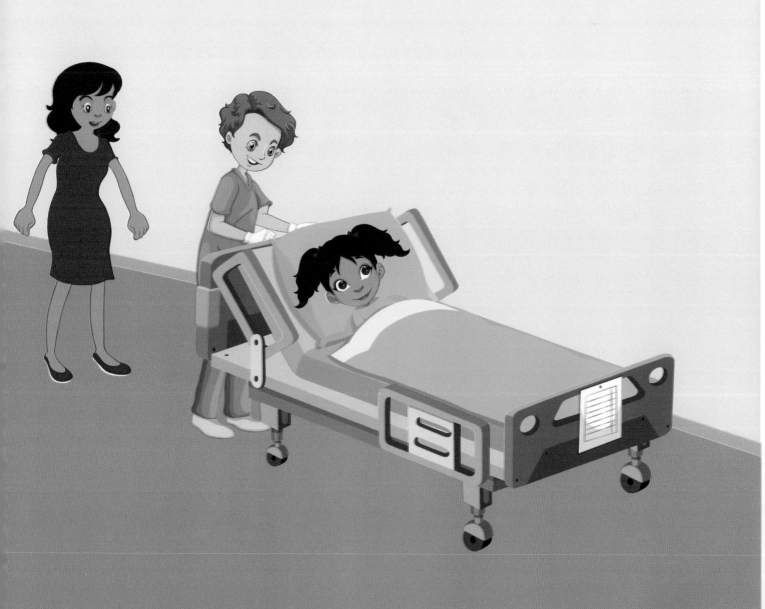

Now another doctor comes to see Alice. It is his job to give Alice some medicine to help with her operation.

He is called an anaesthetist. (An-e–the-tist)

This may be cream on the back of her hand or a few drops of liquid in Alice's IV drip. This medicine makes Alice feel relaxed and calm.

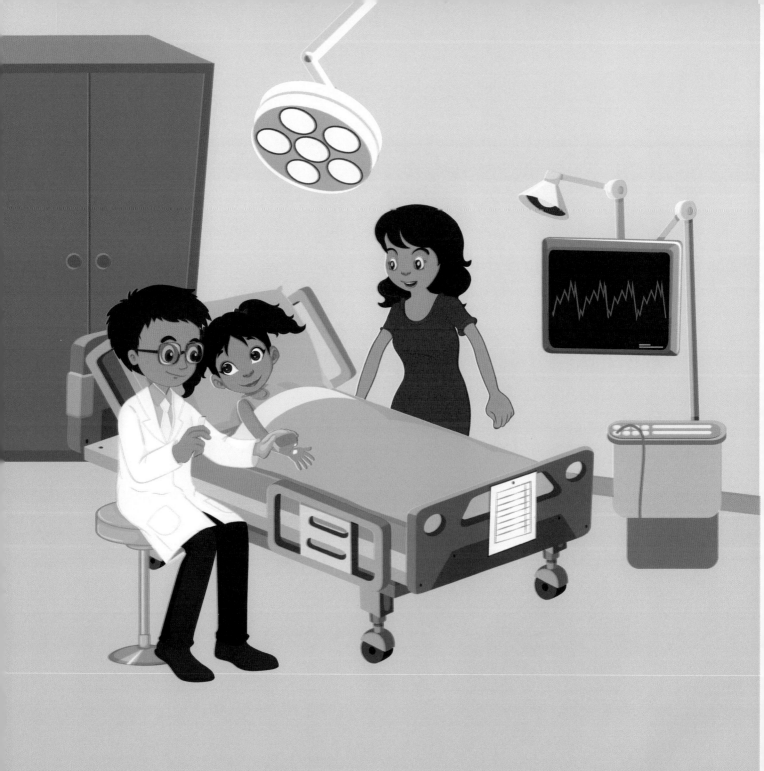

In the operating theatre, there are lots of people who are helping Alice through the operation. The anaesthetist puts a special superhero mask on Alice's face to help her fall asleep. When she wakes up, the operation will be over.

Alice does not see, feel or hear anything while she is having the operation. She sleeps really, really well.

The anaesthetist stays with Alice the whole time, to make sure she is safe.

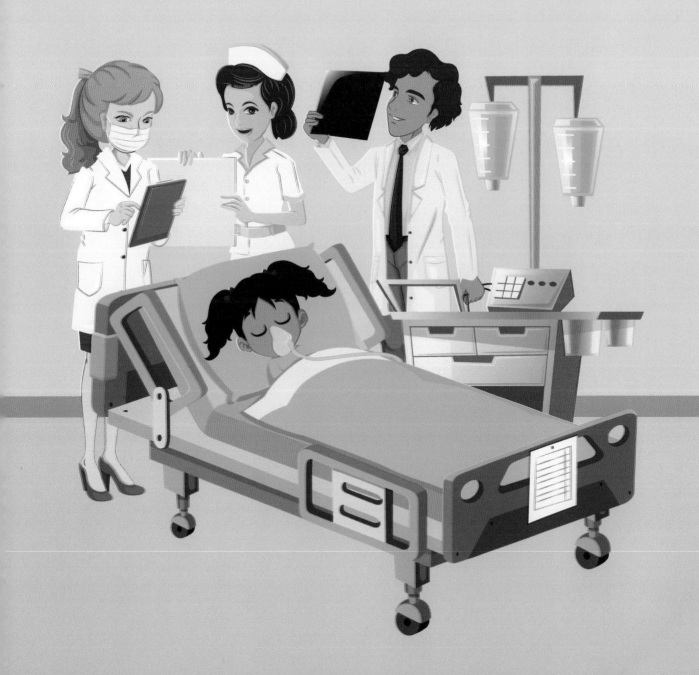

After the operation, Alice wakes up from her big sleep in the recovery room. Mummy and a nurse are there to make sure she is all right.

Alice feels sleepy at first from the medicine she was given before her operation, but she soon wakes up properly.

The nurse gives Alice something to eat and drink and checks how Alice is feeling.

The medicine in Alice's IV drip helps her to feel better.

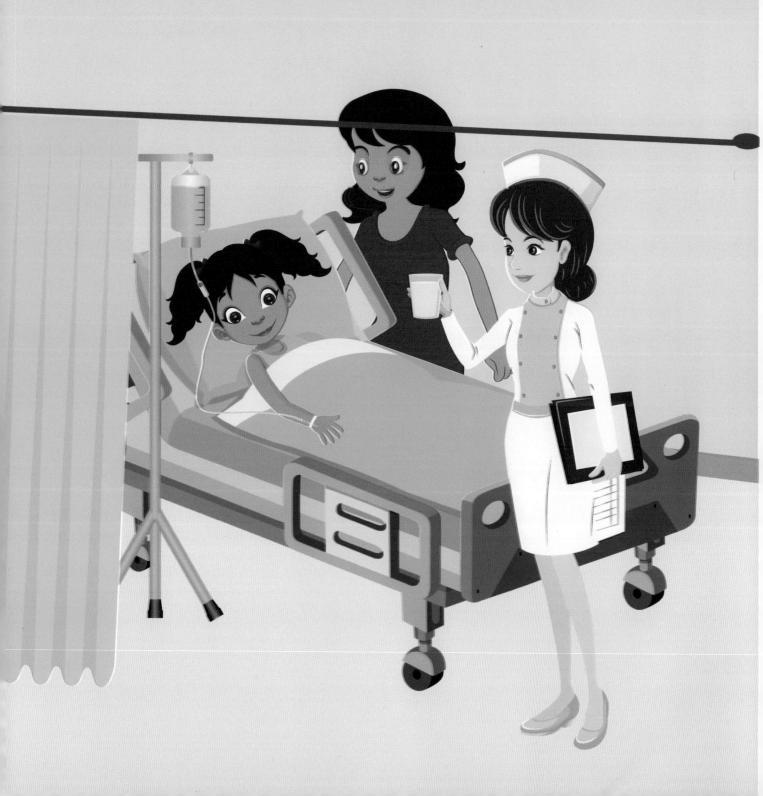

After a little while, the friendly porter takes Alice back to her room in the bed with wheels. She needs to rest.

If she wants to, she can sleep for a little while longer or play with her toys. Mummy can read her a story.

Throughout the day and night, the doctors and nurses come to check that Alice is all right. Mummy stays with her the whole time too.

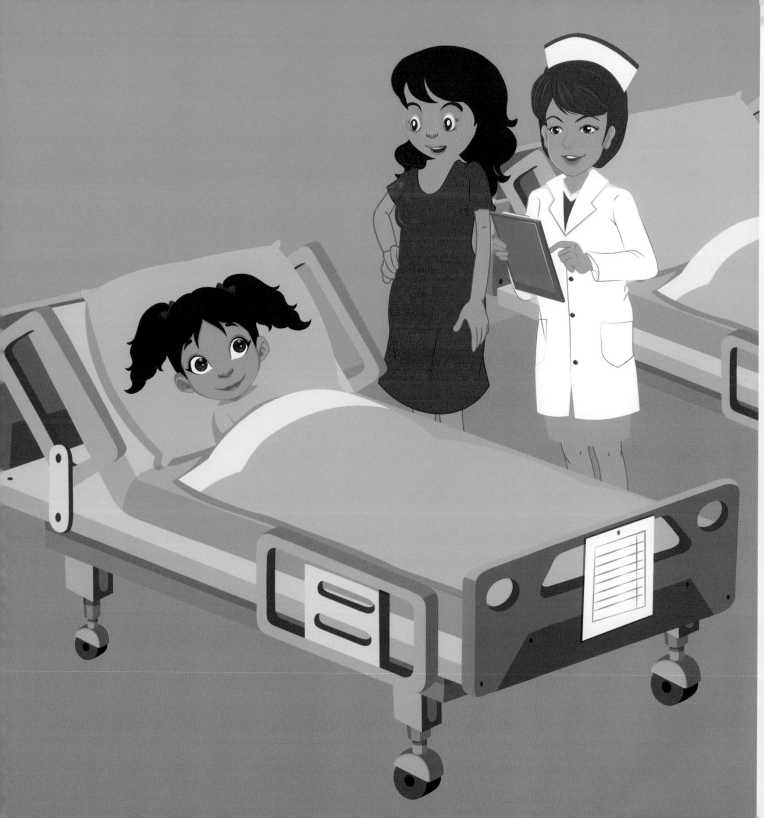

Alice stays in the hospital until she feels a bit better and the doctors and nurses look after her very well.

She makes friends with some of the other children in her ward.

After a couple of days, Alice is feeling much better and is excited about going home.

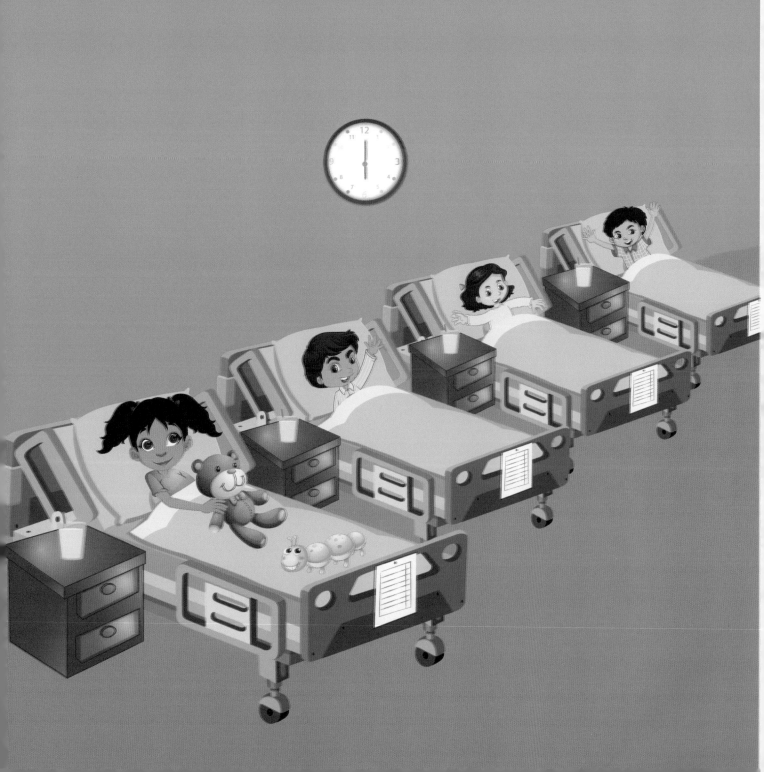

When Alice gets home, she needs to rest for a few days, so she sits on the sofa watching TV and playing quiet games. Her tummy is still a little bit sore, and she feels tired.

A few days later, Alice is feeling much better and can go outside with her brother, Jimmy and her best friend, Tara. She has missed playing with them.

Although she was a little bit scared to go to the hospital, Alice had a wonderful adventure. And best of all, her tummy is no longer sore!

Yay!

Remember, it's okay to feel scared if you have to go to the hospital for an operation.

But with the help of an adult and the kind nurses, doctors, porters, and other people who work there, you will have a safe stay at the hospital.

You will see new things (like big machines).

You will smell new smells, and you will make new friends.

It will be a wonderful adventure!

Other Books by Beanz Book

Ollie's Tonsils

Smelly Melly, Personal Hygiene for Kids and Little Monsters

Printed in Great Britain
by Amazon

23772525R00025